To Rich – JL
To Zohra with love – DA

First published in Great Britain 2016 by Egmont UK Limited
This edition published 2018 by Dean, an imprint of Egmont UK Limited,
The Yellow Building, 1 Nicholas Road, London, W11 4AN
www.egmont.co.uk

ISBN 978 0 6035 7561 7
A CIP catalogue record for this title is available from the British Library.

EGMONT
We bring stories to life

Hooray for Knickers

Jill Lewis
&
Deborah Allwright

EGMONT

King Grouchy
was always grumpy,
so he didn't have many friends.

Even when he was supposed to
be having fun he was still grumpy!

Prince Jolly, however, had lots of friends and the king wanted to be one of them, so he invited him for a swim at the Palace.

King Grouchy wanted everything to be perfect for the visit.

The day came and King Grouchy got out of bed on the wrong side. This put him in a seriously bad mood.

All the servants hid to keep out of his way.

So King Grouchy shouted the order:

"Prince Jolly is coming for a swim!

And he's going to be my new best friend!

We need floats, deck chairs and silky slippers!

Get everything
and get it now!"

The Royal Butler listened hard
from the cupboard under the stairs.

"What?!"

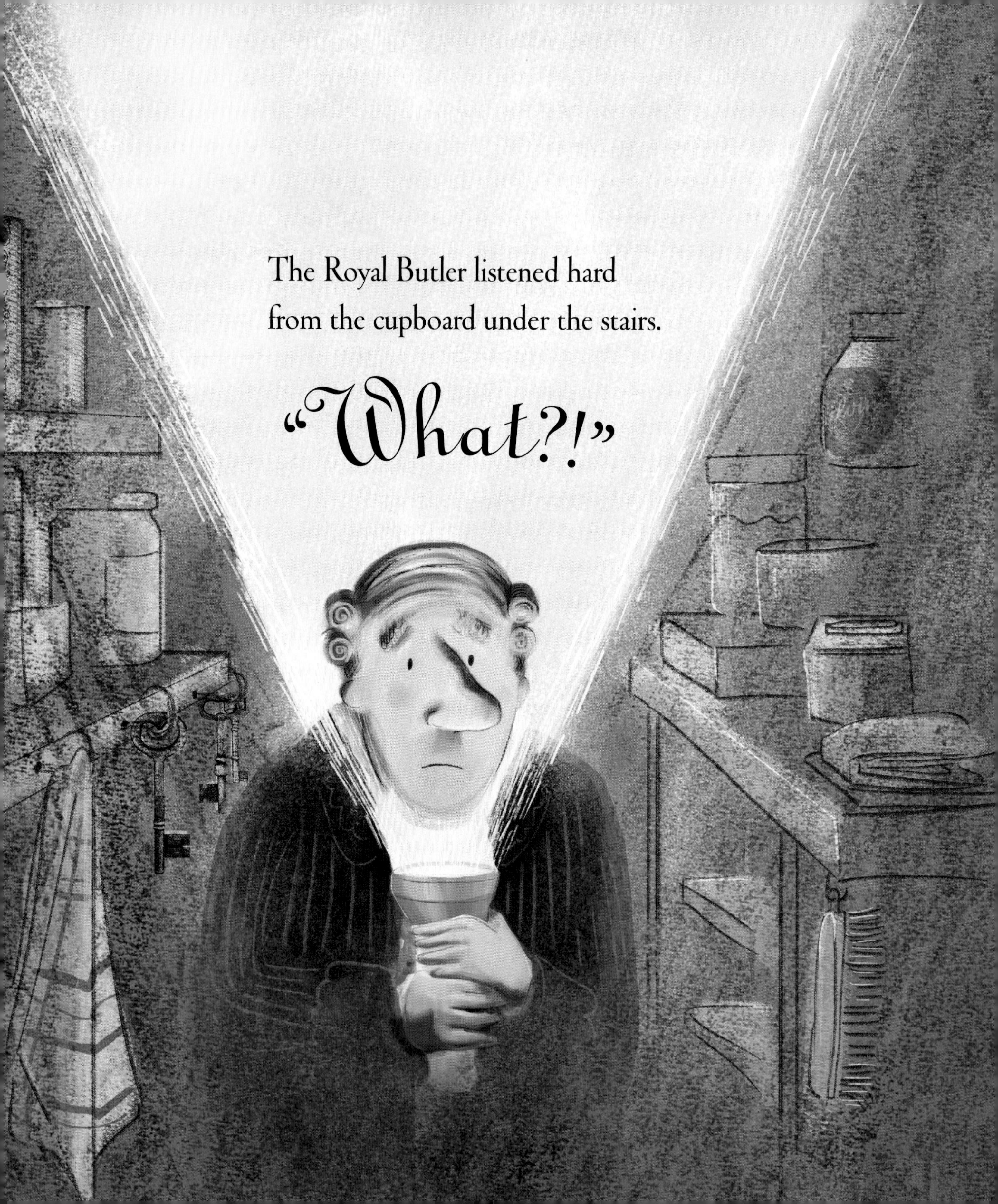

He panicked and yelled the order:

"Prince Jolly is coming for a swim!

He's going to be the king's new best friend. They need boats, black bears and silly flippers.

Help me get everything now!"

The Royal Footman strained to hear from the hayloft.

"What?!"

He panicked and yelled:

"The king's got a new best friend
who's coming for a swim!
They need goats, a sack of pears
and **smelly kippers.**
Help me get everything now!"

The Royal Gardener struggled to hear from the greenhouse.

"*What?!*"

He panicked and yelled:

"The king's best friend in the **world** is coming for a swim. They need coats, stacks of hares and **sparkly stickers.**
Help me get everything now!"

The Royal Maid could hardly hear from behind the washing basket and was puzzled.

"*What?!*" she asked.

"He needs skipping ropes?
A funfair?

And everyone needs
frilly knickers?

Oh well, if that's what the king's best
friend in the whole wide world wants . . ."

At last, Prince Jolly arrived.

"We're going to have a lovely time,"
King Grouchy said proudly. "I've ordered everything we need."
And he led the prince out onto the balcony to show him.

"What?!" Prince Jolly exclaimed.

They looked at…

. . . the boats, the goats, the coats and the ropes.
They gawped at the funfair, the bears,
the pears and the hares.

They gaped at the flippers,
the kippers, the stickers and . . .

. . . all the frilly knickers!

King Grouchy turned redder
and redder and **redder.**

He was about to **explode** when . . .

Prince Jolly burst out laughing!

"I had no idea you have so much fun here," he beamed.

"Best friends need matching frilly knickers and we need them now!"

King Grouchy couldn't believe he
had a best friend. "You're right,"
he chuckled, "we do have fun here.

Hooray for knickers!

. . . Let the party begin!"